# YURI and the Jungle Ribbon

## BY EMMA UGARELLI

Juvenile Fiction Keywords: animal, monkeys,
Amazon rainforest, jungle story, natural habitat,
jungle animals, friendship, kindness.

JUV002020 JUVENILE FICTION/Animal/Apes, Monkeys
JUVU002340 JUVENILE FICTION/Animal/Jungle Animals,
Amazon, Environment, Nature
JUVU3922 JUVENILE FICTION/Social Themes/Values and Virtues


ISBN: 978-1-7386963-7-6 (Hardcover)
ISBN: 978-1-7386963-6-9 (Paperback)
ISBN: 978-1-7386963-8-3 (eBook)

This book is dedicated to my family, my children, and my mom, who is my guide and example.

To my beloved Peru.

Yuri was walking in the jungle
when something fell - **plop!**
- on his head.

"**Ouch!**" Yuri looked up to see who or what hit him. "Where are you? Show your face!" yelled Yuri, but nobody answered.

He looked at the ground, and there was **the culprit!** A round, shiny, hard object. "What could this be?"

Yuri grabbed it, looked at it closely, and then bit it so hard that it chipped his teeth. "Owww!"

Jaguar noticed Yuri and curiously asked,
"What are you doing with a COIN, Yuri?"

"**AHH!**" Yuri gasped. "Is this a thing
humans use to buy stuff?"

"Yes!" nodded Jaguar.
Yuri was excited. "I can buy whatever I like, **YAY!**"

"Buy bananas," advised Jaguar.
"Bananas? No! Why would I buy bananas
when I could climb a tree for them?" Yuri argued.

"Then buy **CANDY!** I love candy!" Jaguar drooled.
"**Nooo!** It will not last and will crack
my teeth; too much sugar."

At that moment, Yuri saw some kids
playing, and a girl with a beautiful string
on her head caught his attention.

"Oh, I've got it! I'm going to buy **that**," Yuri said.
Then he added, "It will make me look so pretty."

"That is a **ribbon**," said Jaguar.
"You need to go to the store for one of those."

Without thinking twice, Yuri ran as fast as he could toward the closest store.

He looked around until he finally found a colourful ribbon inside a box.

Yuri took the ribbon,
left his money on the
counter, and ran back
to the shore.

He couldn't wait to try it on, but he didn't know
how to place the ribbon on his head.

When he tried it, his hands and feet got tied up.

"ARGH!"

Luckily, a girl named Nina saw
Yuri all tangled up and came to his rescue.

"What are you trying to do?" she asked, smiling.

Yuri shook his arms, trying to show Nina
how he wanted the ribbon.

**"Ah!** I see. Try not to move," she said.

After untangling Yuri, Nina asked, "Do you want the ribbon on your hand?"

Yuri shook his head. **NO!**

"Do you want it on your waist?" Yuri shook his head hard. **NO! NO!**

"Do you want it on your neck?" Yuri shook his head even harder. **NO! NO! NO!**

Yuri pointed at Nina's ribbon. "Oh! Do you want it on your head?"

Yuri nodded excitedly. **YES!**

When Nina finished, Yuri looked at himself in the
water and jumped happily. "I look awesome!" he cheered.
Then he started walking.

Yuri strolled proudly, moving his head from left to right, showing off his new look.

His friends looked at him and his ribbon with surprise.

**"Well?"** asked Yuri, "What do you think?"

Everybody praised his ribbon, and Yuri was pleased.
But after some time, a friend said, "Let's go play!"

The others excitedly replied, "YES!"
**"OH NO!"** cried Yuri, who wanted to continue
being the centre of attention.

"Well, I'm staying here."

As the days passed, Yuri kept refusing to play; he made up excuses, telling his friends he couldn't play because he was sick. *COUGH, COUGH!*

But the truth was that he did not want to **LOSE** his ribbon.

After a while, his friends stopped asking him to play, and he started to feel lonely.

He was **PRETTIER** than before but not **HAPPIER** than before. He had something nobody had but nobody to talk to about it.

Yuri thought that his ribbon was enough. *But is it?* he wondered.

One day while Yuri was feeling lonely, he followed his friends to watch them play.

Suddenly, he heard a commotion. Everybody was yelling!
He heard someone shout, "**Help me! Please!**"

Yuri quickly moved to where the call for help had come from.
He was shocked to see that little Emmy had fallen into the river!
*I must do something*, thought Yuri.

Without a second thought,
Yuri took the ribbon from his head.

He tied one end to a tree and the other to his waist before
jumping into the river to rescue his little friend.

For a moment, everybody froze; they could not see Yuri or Emmy! But then...

Everybody **CHEERED** as Yuri emerged from the water with Emmy in his arms.

When Yuri's friends saw the ribbon, they cried, "Oh NO! Your ribbon, Yuri! It is ruined."

Yuri shrugged his shoulders. "It's okay. A good friend is more valuable than anything I could ever have."

"Let's play!" Yuri said. "I have a new game for us to try."

"What is it?" asked his friends.

YURI excitedly said, "Let's hide the ...**RIBBON!**"

Thank you so much for reading. I hope you enjoyed this book—and if you did, please consider leaving an honest review on Goodreads, Amazon, or my website: www.eugarellibooks.com.

Please check out my other books, *Lou and His Mane*, *Yuri and the Treasure Box*, and *Kenny and His Great Invention*, and visit my website www.eugarellibooks.com for activities, games, and news.

*- Emma Ugarelli*

Made in the USA
Monee, IL
30 June 2023

38019605R00019